THE SIX SWANS

For our sister Ellen

With love and appreciation

From Bob and Dan

SIMON AND SCHUSTER
BOOKS FOR YOUNG READERS
Simon & Schuster Building
Rockefeller Center
1230 Avenue of the Americas
New York, New York 10020

10 9 8 7 6 5 4 3 2 1

Library of Congress Cataloging-in-Publication Data
San Souci, Robert.
The six swans/retold by Robert D. San Souci; illustrated by
Daniel San Souci.   p. cm.
SUMMARY: A retelling of how the king's daughter rescues her six
brothers from the enchantment imposed on them by their wicked
stepmother.
[1. Fairy tales.   2. Folklore—Germany.]   I. San Souci, Daniel, ill.   II. Title.
PZ8.S248Si 1989
398.2′1′0943—dc19
[E]   88-11375   CIP   AC
ISBN 0–671–65848–4

Robert D. San Souci's

THE SIX SWANS

Illustrated by Daniel San Souci

SIMON AND SCHUSTER BOOKS FOR YOUNG READERS

Published by Simon & Schuster Inc., New York

ne day a king went hunting in an enchanted forest, pursuing a magnificent stag so eagerly that his huntsmen could not keep up. The creature led him deeper and deeper into the wood, then suddenly vanished. Puzzled, the king reined in his horse and looked around him. He realized that he had lost his way, and evening was falling. On all sides, he heard the snarls and growls of strange beasts roaming in the shadows.

Vainly, he searched for a way out of the wood, but the path he had followed had disappeared as surely as the deer. He found another path and followed it for a while. Soon he saw an old woman, coming toward him. She leaned on a staff of hazelwood that went *Tap! Tap! Tap!* as she approached.

"Good woman," he called, "can you show me the way out of this forest?"

"I can easily show you the way—but only upon one condition," the woman said. "If you don't agree to it, you'll never get out of the wood."

"What is the condition?" asked the king uneasily.

"I have a daughter," said the old woman, "who is so beautiful, only a king is worthy of her. If you will promise to marry her, and make her your queen, I will show you the way out of the forest."

Horrible creatures were moving all about the darkening forest now. The king, certain that he would never escape without the old woman's help, agreed to her condition. He had guessed that this was an enchanted wood, and that the old woman was a witch.

Laughing to herself, the woman led him to a fine house in the heart of the wood. Inside, they found her daughter sitting at the fireside. The young woman greeted the king as though she were expecting him. He saw that she was very beautiful indeed, but her eyes glittered like a spider's, and the dancing flames made her shadow look squat and misshapen. He could not look at her without feeling a secret dislike.

But he had given his word. So he lifted the maiden upon his horse, seating her behind him. Then the old woman showed him the path that led beyond the forest.

So the king reached his palace, where he proceeded to marry the woman.

Now the king had been married once before, and his first wife had died. She had given him seven children—six boys and a girl—whom he loved more than the whole world. But their new stepmother took an immediate dislike to them, and the king was afraid that she might harm them. So, one night, he took them secretly to a lonely castle in the midst of a wood. The place was so hidden that the king himself could only find it because a wise woman had given him a magic ball of golden thread. When he threw this on the ground, it unwound itself, running ahead to show him the path. When he wished to return, he followed the thread as it rewound itself.

The new queen tried and tried to learn the whereabouts of her stepchildren. Finally, she bribed a servant with gold, and he told her the secret of the hidden castle and the magic ball of thread.

She did not rest until she found where the king had hidden the magic thread. Then she sewed some little shirts of white silk. Into each she wove a white swan's feather over which she whispered some magic words her mother had taught her.

The next time the king went hunting, she took the little shirts and the ball of golden thread, and went into the wood. There the magic thread showed her the way to the secret castle.

When the little boys saw someone coming, they thought it was their father, and ran out joyfully to greet him. Then the queen threw the little shirts over them. As soon as the shirts touched their bodies, they were changed into swans who flew away over the treetops.

With a gleeful cry, the wicked queen turned and followed the thread back the way she had come, thinking she was rid of her stepchildren forever.

But the boys' sister had not run out with her brothers, and the queen did not know that she had escaped the spell.

The next day, the king came to the castle to visit his children, but he found his daughter all alone.

"Where are your brothers?" asked the king.

"Alas!" she cried, "they have been changed into swans. From the window, I saw them fly away over the wood."

The king was beside himself with grief, unable to imagine who had done this wicked deed. At last he said, "In the morning, we will return to my palace." Though he feared the girl's stepmother, he was more afraid that his last child would be stolen away if she remained in the castle in the wood.

But the young woman thought to herself, "My father is so sad, and I miss my brothers so, that I will go and look for them."

When night fell, and her father slept, she ran away into the wood. For a night and a day she wandered, until she was ready to drop from weariness. Then, as the day drew to a close, she came to a fine house in a clearing.

She knocked politely. When no one answered, she went in and up the stairs. At the top, she found a room with six little beds in it. Not daring to lie down in any of them, she crept under one and stretched herself out on the hard floor to rest for the night.

But soon afterward, as the sun was going down, she heard a rustling noise, and saw six swans come flying in the window. They arranged themselves in a circle on the floor. To the girl, it seemed that the image of the swans shimmered, as if she were looking at them reflected in a pool of rippling water. Then, she was no longer looking at six swans, but at her six lost brothers.

With a cry of joy, she scrambled from under the bed and embraced them. Her brothers were just as happy to see her, but their joy did not last long.

"You can't stay here," her oldest brother said. "This is the house of a wicked witch, who is also an ogress. If she comes home and finds you here, she will make you a swan, too."

"Then run away with me at once," she urged.

"No," said another brother, "we can only return to human form an hour each evening. For that brief time we are boys again, but then we turn back into swans."

"Oh, my poor brothers," wept the girl, "isn't there some way to break this spell?"

"Alas! No!" said her youngest brother. "The conditions are too hard."

"For six long years you must neither speak nor laugh," said another.

"During that time," said the third, "you must make for us six shirts—each a different color—sewn of tiny dew-flowers."

"These are only found in the meadow at the edge of the forest," added the fourth, "and can be picked only at the first light of dawn."

"When the shirts are finished, cast them upon us, and we will be free of the spell," said the fifth brother.

"But if you laugh even once, or utter a single word, all of your labor is lost," the eldest boy warned, "and we will remain swans forever."

But the little maiden vowed, "I will set you free, even if it should cost me my life."

The moment she said this, their hour was up, and the boys changed back into swans. Away they flew, out the window. The last to leave said, "Follow the trail we will show you."

Then, hearing the *Tap! Tap! Tap!* of the witch's staff upon the path (for it was the same house her father had been brought to not long before,) she slipped away into the woods. There she followed a trail of feathers the swans had let fall to the edge of the woods. Then she curled up in the roots of a tree and slept through the night.

At morning's first light, the girl went hunting dew-flowers. But she was able to find only a few of the tiny, rainbow-colored blossoms—each bright as a jewel and no bigger than a dewdrop—before the rising sun turned the unpicked flowers to mist and they faded away.

Taking the few she had gathered, the girl climbed into a comfortable fork in a tree, and began to sew. She could not talk to anyone, and she had no reason to laugh, so she sat quietly at her needle, and never once took her eyes from her work.

She had been sewing for a long time, when it happened that the king of that country went hunting in the wood one day. Some of his huntsmen chanced upon the tree in which the girl was sitting.

"Who are you?" they called up to her.

But she gave no answer.

"Come down," they said. "We won't hurt you."

She only shook her head.

But they went on, teasing her with questions. So she threw down her golden necklace, thinking that would satisfy them. But they did not stop asking her questions, so she threw down her ring and her embroidered belt.

But they would not be put off. They climbed the tree, lifted the young woman down, and brought her to the king.

"Who are you? What were you doing up in the tree?" the king asked her in all the languages he knew, but she did not answer. She merely stood, holding the dew-flowers and a tiny bit of the first shirt in her apron.

The king thought her the most beautiful creature he had ever seen, and fell deeply in love with her at once. He wrapped his royal cloak around her, set her upon his horse, and brought her to his palace.

There he ordered her clothed in a rich gown, and she shone in her beauty like the bright day. But no one could coax a word or a smile from her.

The king set her beside him at his table, and announced to his court, "This is the maiden I am going to marry."

Their wedding took place a few days afterward. In the days that followed, the new queen used every moment she could spare to seek the rare, magical dew-flowers and sew the shirts that would free her brothers.

Now the king had a wicked aunt, who was none other than the witch of the wood. When she guessed who the girl was, she pounded her staff on the floor angrily. "Who knows who she is or where she comes from?" she said to the king and all the court. "The king's wife might be an ogress in disguise, for all we know!"

But the king was so in love with his wife, he paid no attention.

At the end of the year, when the queen brought her first child—a little girl—into the world, the old witch spirited the infant away. Then she went to the king, crying, "She has done something terrible with the child. She is surely an ogress!"

But the king would not believe this, and would not allow any harm to come to his wife.

The innocent queen was torn between fear for her child and her vow to rescue her brothers. In the evening, she sat in her room, trying to sew, but her eyes were so filled with tears, she couldn't see to finish a stitch.

Suddenly, she heard the rustle of wings at the window. Then a swan landed on the window ledge. It was one of her swan-brothers.

"Have no fear," said the swan, "your child is safe in our keeping. But you can't see her until the spell upon us is broken."

Then he flew away into the twilight.

So the young queen kept silently sewing at the shirts.

The next time, when she had a fine little boy, the wicked old aunt stole the baby, and again accused the queen of being an ogress.

But the king said, "She is too good and gentle to be capable of such a thing. If she could speak for herself, she would prove her innocence."

Once again, one of her brothers, in the guise of a swan, came to her and said, "Your child is safe in our keeping, until the spell is broken."

The third time the queen had a little child, the old witch stole the baby girl away with magic, and accused the queen as before.

The queen, as always, would not say one word in her own defense. This time, there was such an outcry among the nobles and common folk, that the king was forced to let his wife be judged in the court. There, the witch used lies and gold to get her way, and the queen was sentenced to death.

Now it happened that the day on which she was to die was also the last day of the six years during which she was neither to speak nor laugh. In her prison cell, she had finished the six flower shirts, except that the last one lacked the left sleeve.

Clutching these to her heart, she was led out to the place of execution. Just as the king, her husband, went to embrace her one last time, there came the flutter of wings high above.

Swooping down through the air came six swans, two-by-two,

each pair supporting a basket with one of the queen's beautiful
babies. They alighted gently on the ground in front of her, and she
tossed the shirts over them—red, yellow, green, blue, orange and
purple.

The minute the dew-flower shirts touched them, her brothers
stood before her in their natural form, whole and handsome. Only
the youngest, over whom the unfinished shirt had fallen, had a
swan's wing instead of his left arm.

Laughing with joy, the queen gathered up her infants and hugged and kissed her brothers. Then she said to the king, who was lost in amazement, "Dearest husband, at last I can speak; and I swear to you, I have been falsely accused."

She told him how his wicked aunt had used her magic to spirit away their three children. Then the king ordered the witch put to death, but she turned herself into a raven that flew screeching into the air.

Quickly the king grabbed a crossbow and shot the bird and that was the end of the witch.

Then the queen and her brothers went to visit their father in his distant kingdom. When their wicked stepmother saw that her magic had been undone, she became so angry she turned into the ogress she really was, and ran howling into the wood, never to be seen again.

And so the young king and queen and all their loved ones lived many years in peace and happiness.